To

........Lyla........,
MERRY CHRISTMAS!
Love from
........Mimi & Papa........ (2022)

Gingerbread Town

.....Lyla..... sees a present
wrapped up neatly with a bow.
The label has a name,
and the wrapping seems to glow.

"This present is for me!" cries ....Lyla........,
with the biggest grin.

....Lyla.......... opens it to look inside,
and suddenly falls in!

Lyla

is in the frosty woods,
looking at blue skies.
To find a world inside a box
is such a big surprise!

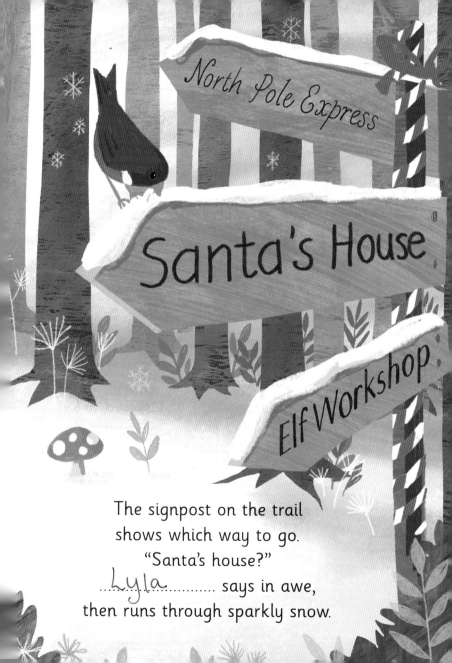

North Pole Express

Santa's House

Elf Workshop

The signpost on the trail
shows which way to go.
"Santa's house?"
.....Lyla.......... says in awe,
then runs through sparkly snow.

......Lyla...... spots a village
and a family up ahead.
......Lyla........ gasps and can't believe,
they're made of gingerbread!

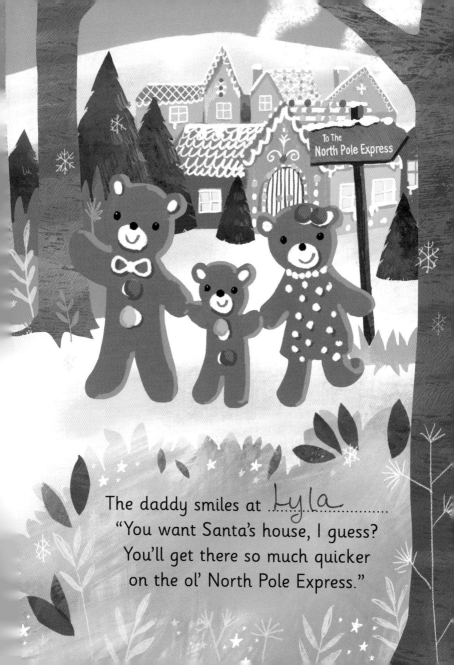

The daddy smiles at Lyla
"You want Santa's house, I guess?
You'll get there so much quicker
on the ol' North Pole Express."

.....Lyla.......... is at the station
and spots a little elf.
The elf exclaims, "I'm off to see
Santa Claus, himself."

.....Lyla..... is excited.
"Yes, I'm off to see him too!
But I'm not sure which way to go.
Can I come along with you?"

They hear a distant chugging sound,
then see the train appear.
The elf says, "..........._Lyla_.........., this is it!
The North Pole Express is here!"

A small penguin conductor
brings the steam train to a stop.
"All aboard!" he shouts to Lyla.
"Come ride with me up top."

..........Lyla.......... has the perfect seat
and an even better view.
Snowy forests whiz on by,
while the chimney toots "choo-choo!"

NORTH POLE EXPRESS

Santa's House

They reach their destination.
.......hyla......'s face is full of cheer.
The penguin blows his whistle,
shouting, "Hooray! We are here!"

The elf takes ......Lyla...... to a house.
Mrs. Claus greets them with glee.
"I'm so glad you are here at last.
Come in and sit with me!"

...........*Leyla*........... sips hot chocolate,
and eats warm cookies from a plate.
The elf says, "...........*Leyla*..........., we must go.
We really can't be late."

.....hyla..... is led through
a busy workshop full of elves,
where a million shiny toys
sit high on countless shelves.

"Will I see Santa?" _Lyla_ hopes.
"I think that would be neat."
The elf says, "Yes! That's why you're here.
He really wants to meet!"

"Ho ho hello, ...Lyla.....!
You've been sooo good this year.
That's why I left a magic gift—
so I could bring you here!"

"Yes, you wished to meet me.
I made that wish come true.
And now, I have a special toy.
One I made…just for you."

....Lyla........ peeks inside the box.
What could this present be?
Santa magically disappears,
and ....Lyla........ is by the tree.

The trip has been amazing,
a night ......Lyla...... won't forget.
And in the box is Santa's gift:
a North Pole Express train set!

Merry
Christmas

Lyla........, hop on board the
NORTH POLE EXPRESS!

Draw yourself and your friends
on the train to see Santa.

Written by J.D. Green
Illustrated by Joanne Partis
Designed by Ryan Dunn

Put Me In The Story is a
registered trademark of Sourcebooks, Inc.
All rights reserved.

Published by Put Me In The Story,
a publication of Sourcebooks.
P.O. Box 4410, Naperville, Illinois 60567-4410
(630) 536-1104
www.putmeinthestory.com

Date of Production: June 2022
Run Number: 5025359
Printed and bound in Italy (LG)
10 9 8 7 6 5 4 3 2 1

MIX
Paper from
responsible sources
FSC® C023419
FSC
www.fsc.org

put me
in the story®
Bestselling books starring your child!
www.putmeinthestory.com